SCREAM STREET

Book Eleven

HUNGER OF THE YETI

WITHDRAWN

The fiendish fun continues at
www.screamstreet.com

SCREAM STREET

Book Eleven
HUNGER OF THE YETI

TOMMY D⊙NBAVAND

CANDLEWICK PRESS

Text copyright © 2011 by Tommy Donbavand
Illustrations copyright © 2011 by Cartoon Saloon Ltd.

First U.S. edition 2015

Library of Congress Catalog Card Number 2014945723
ISBN 978-0-7636-5763-5

15 16 17 18 19 20 FRS 10 9 8 7 6 5 4 3 2 1

Printed in Altona, Manitoba, Canada

This book was typeset in Bembo Educational.
The illustrations were done in ink.

Candlewick Press
99 Dover Street
Somerville, Massachusetts 02144

visit us at www.candlewick.com

For Layla and Cassie

Meet the residents

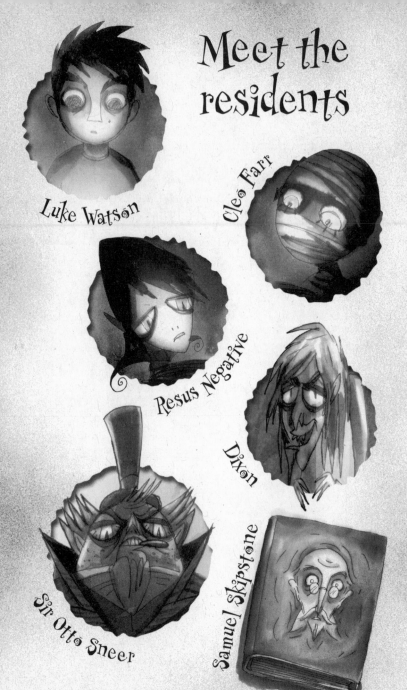

Luke Watson

Cleo Farr

Resus Negative

Dixon

Sir Otto Sneer

Samuel Skipstone

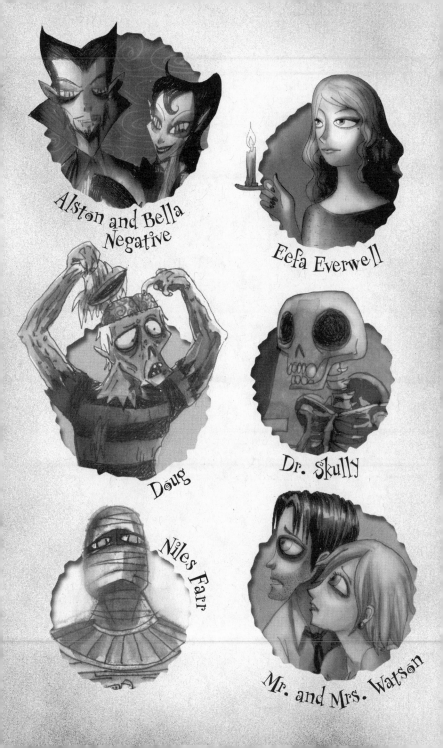

Alston and Bella Negative

Eefa Everwell

Doug

Dr. Skully

Niles Farr

Mr. and Mrs. Watson

Who lives where

A Sneer Hall

B Central Square

C Everwell's Emporium

D No. 2: The Crudlegs

E No. 5: The Movers

F No. 11: Twinkle

G No. 13: Luke Watson

H No. 14: Resus Negative

I No. 21: Eefa Everwell

J No. 22: Cleo Farr

K No. 26: The Headless
Horseman

L No. 27: Femur Ribs

M No. 28: Doug, Turf,
and Berry

N No. 31: Kian Negative

O No. 32: Ryan Aire

P No. 39: The Skullys

Previously on Scream Street...

Mr. and Mrs. Watson were terrified when their son, Luke, first transformed into a werewolf. But that was nothing compared to their terror at being forcibly moved to Scream Street—and discovering there was no going back.

Determined to take his parents home, Luke enlisted the help of his new friends, Resus Negative, a wannabe vampire, and Cleo Farr, an Egyptian mummy, to find six relics left behind by the community's founding fathers. Only by collecting these magical artifacts would he be able to open a doorway back to his own world.

Just as Luke and his friends finally succeeded in their quest, Mr. and Mrs. Watson realized how happy Luke had become in his new home and decided to stay on in Scream Street. But the newly opened doorway was becoming a problem—Sir Otto Sneer, Scream Street's wicked landlord, was charging "normals" from Luke's world to visit what he called "the world's greatest freak show."

To protect Scream Street, Luke, Resus, and Cleo must try to close the doorway by returning the relics to their original owners—and a zombie's tongue is next on the list....

Chapter One
The Mountain

The vampire's cape whipped out behind him in the wind, flashes of the electric-blue lining standing out against the stark gray mountainside. Gritting his fangs against the cold wind, he marched on, his shiny leather shoes sending a mini avalanche of rocks and pebbles cascading down the slope below. Then—and not for the first time that morning—a snowball exploded against the back of his head.

"You know, that's getting very boring very quickly," Resus Negative moaned to his giggling friends. "Plus, I'm cold enough without the extra snow down my neck, thank you very much!"

"It's your own fault that you're cold." Luke Watson grinned. "You're not dressed for this kind of weather. I did offer to lend you my spare hiking boots. . . ."

Resus gestured to his crisp, clean shirt and dress-suit pants. "You honestly think I'm going to wear boots with this?" he asked. "I'd look stupid!"

"You look stupid *now*— and freezing," replied Luke, pushing his hands deep into the pockets of his heavy winter coat.

"And you don't know what you're missing," added Cleo Farr as she bounded past in the extra hiking boots. "This stuff is *so* comfortable!" The young mummy was wearing a woolen hat, a thick sweater, and a pair of Luke's mom's jeans.

Resus pulled his cloak around him and shivered. "There's no need to rub it in," he grumbled. "How was I supposed to know Tibet would be so cold?"

"There must be something in your cape that could keep you warm without making you look like an idiot," Cleo insisted. Resus plunged his hand into his cloak and produced a pair of knitted baby booties and a Santa hat.

"Then again, maybe not . . ."

"It can't be far now," said Luke, studying a crude map scribbled on the back of an envelope. "The old woman in the village said Vein's cave was just up here."

"That's another thing," snapped Resus, putting the hat and booties away again. "What's a zombie doing living at the top of a mountain? It's not natural."

"The villagers say he's their local soothsayer," explained Cleo.

"Sooth-what?"

"Soothsayer," repeated Luke. "Someone who can predict the future."

"Ridiculous," scoffed Resus.

"It's not ridiculous," Cleo retorted. "Back in Egypt, we had soothsayers who predicted everything from how well the next year's crops would grow to who would be buried alongside the pharaoh in his tomb."

"Sounds fishy to me," Resus said. "And even if Vein *can* see the future, how does he manage to tell people what's going to happen to them? He's got no tongue!"

Luke smiled. He had to admit, Resus did have a point. Vein was one of Scream Street's founding fathers, and he'd given the trio his tongue—a powerful relic—so that Luke could open a doorway out of the community and take his parents back to their own world. At the time, the zombie had been the lead singer of the popular flesh-metal band Brain Drain. The latest news was that the band had split up and Vein had hidden himself away here in Tibet.

"I'm sure he'll explain everything after we return his tongue," Luke said, running his fingers over the box in his pocket containing the lump of flesh.

"But we can't give it back until we find him," Cleo reminded them. "And standing here chatting isn't going to help us do that. Come on!" She strode confidently ahead, gripping the larger rocks to pull herself up the bleak hillside.

Luke laughed. "She's eager," he said.

"She's annoying," retorted Resus.

"I don't think she's been anywhere quite like this before," said Luke. "After spending most of her life trapped inside a pyramid, somewhere like this must be a bit of an advent—"

"HELP!"

The cry pierced the cold air, echoing off the neighboring mountain. Luke and Resus looked up ahead to where the sound had come from. Cleo had vanished from sight.

"What's she gone and done now?" huffed Resus, beginning to set off at a run.

"She didn't listen, that's what!" replied Luke, catching him up. "Mr. Chillchase warned us to stay together."

"Since when did she ever listen to warnings? Or advice? Or anything, really?"

Reaching the spot where they had last seen their friend, Luke and Resus paused to catch their breath and look around. They were standing in the middle of what appeared to be a circle of large stones. Dead leaves and clumps of gray fur whirled around their feet in the chill breeze.

"Look!" hissed Luke. Footprints in the snow trailed across the circle, and draped over one of the rocks was Cleo's scarf.

Resus dashed across the circle to retrieve it but tripped and crashed to the ground. Luke

hurried to where his friend had fallen and stared
in horror.

"Bigfoot!"

Resus pulled himself up onto his knees. "OK,
so we've established that my shoes aren't the best
for mountain climbing, but I wouldn't say they
were particularly large."

"I don't mean you!" said Luke. "Look at what
you tripped over."

The vampire shuffled backward on his knees
and examined the large indentation in the snow.
"That's . . . That's a footprint!" He gasped. "But
it's massive! I know your spare boots were a bit
big for Cleo, but that's ridiculous."

"Cleo didn't make that footprint," said Luke.
"That was made by a yeti."

"Yeti?"

Luke nodded. "Yeti, Bigfoot, the Abominable
Snowman—whatever you want to call them.
They're supposed to live here in Tibet."

"But yetis aren't real," said Resus, standing up again. "They're made-up, mythical creatures."

"I'd have said the same thing about vampires a year ago," Luke pointed out, then a second cry reached them.

"HELP ME!"

The boys raced across the stone ring, stopping abruptly when they realized there was a sheer drop on the other side. Peering cautiously over the edge, Luke could just about see Cleo standing on a small outcrop of rock a few yards below.

"There she is." He sighed. "Come on. . . ."

Easing themselves over the edge, the boys lowered themselves down to where Cleo was standing. Resus glanced anxiously over the side. The ground swam in and out of focus several miles below. "She never gets into trouble near a nice comfortable sofa, does she?" he commented as he and Luke inched furtively toward their friend.

"At last!" Cleo grumbled when they eventually reached her. "I can't get this thing away from me."

The boys stared in amazement. Cleo was backed up against the rock face with what appeared to be an angry gray teddy bear at her feet. The creature snarled and hissed at her.

7

Grrll! Ksst! Grrll!

"What *is* that?" demanded Resus.

"That's a yeti," replied Luke. "I told you they were real—although I have to admit I'd always pictured them bigger than that."

As if it knew it was being talked about, the creature flashed bright red eyes at Luke and Resus, then turned its attention back to Cleo. It only came up to her knees, but what it lacked in size, it made up for in fury.

Ksst! Grrll!

"I think it must be a baby," said Cleo. "I heard it when I was examining that stone-circle thing up there, so I climbed down to get a better look."

Luke rolled his eyes. "Of course you did."

"It looked scared! I came down to see if it was OK, but then it tried to bite me."

Grrll! Grrll!

Cleo flapped her hand at the baby yeti. "Go away! Shoo!"

The creature snapped at her fingers with sharp, pointed teeth, ripping a chunk out of her glove. Torn bandage could be seen through the hole.

"Ow!" yelled Cleo, pulling her hand away. "That hurt!"

"Then stop trying to touch it!" cried Luke.

"I wasn't trying to *touch* it," snapped Cleo. "I was trying to scare it away."

"How? By letting it know how tasty you are?"

"This is ridiculous," groaned Resus. "If you want to get rid of the thing, you *really* have to scare it!" He picked up a small stone and threw it at the yeti, striking it on the leg. The creature dropped to the ground and began to squeal.

Sweeeeeeee! Sweeeeeeeee!

Cleo spun around to glare at the vampire. "Why did you do that?"

"Why do you think?" barked Resus. "I was saving *you*!"

"You didn't have to hurt it."

Sweeeeeeeee! Sweeeeeeeee!

Resus glared at her. "You two have been throwing stuff at me all morning, but as soon as I do the same—"

"The same?" snapped Cleo. "We were throwing snowballs, not rocks!"

GRRRRAAAAWWWLLL!

"What was that?" asked Luke.

"It wasn't a rock," retorted Resus, ignoring him. "It was a pebble—and I didn't throw it hard enough to do any damage."

"Try telling that to the poor little thing. Just look at it!"

Sweeeeeeeee! Sweeeeeeeee!

GRRRRAAAAWWWLLL!

Luke looked over the ledge to see where the new sound was coming from, and he paled. Clambering up the mountainside toward them was a huge mound of gray fur, teeth, and claws. "Er, guys . . ." he said. "I think we've got a bit of a problem. . . ."

Chapter Two
The Rescue

GRRRRAAAAWWWLLL!

The cry of the adult yeti rang loudly in Luke's ears. He looked on nervously as the beast stabbed its claws into the mountainside and climbed toward them.

GRRRRAAAAWWWLLL!

When the baby heard the sound, it leaped back to its feet and began to run madly around the ledge, gnashing its teeth and growling angrily at the newcomers. *Grrll! Grrll! Grrll!*

"Look," Cleo said to Resus. "You've made him really angry now!"

"*He's* not exactly the problem anymore," Luke pointed out. "Come on. We'd better get out of here before his mom reaches us."

GRRRRAAAAWWWLLL!

"Definitely one of your better ideas," Resus agreed, shuddering as the angry creature drew closer.

The trio shuffled back along the thin outcrop, the baby yeti still snapping at their heels. Behind them, a large hairy paw appeared and the creature's mother began to haul herself onto the ledge.

GRRRRAAAAWWWLLL!

Luke cupped his hands to give first Cleo, then Resus a leg up onto the slope above. "Quick!" he hissed urgently.

Grrll! Grrll! Ksst! Ksst!

The baby danced excitedly as its mother appeared beside it on the ledge and raised herself up to her full height. Luke glanced over his shoulder. The yeti was at least nine feet tall and towered over him, her eyes blazing red and saliva dripping from her thick, yellow teeth as she roared at him menacingly.

GRRRRAAAAWWWLLL!

Resus and Cleo dropped to their stomachs, stretching their arms back down toward their friend. Luke could hear the yeti stomping closer as he grabbed their hands and they began to pull him up. A massive paw swung out, just clipping the sole of his hiking boot as he was dragged to safety.

Scrambling to their feet, the trio took up positions in the middle of the stone circle. Resus felt around inside his cape and produced a metal poker and a cricket bat for him and Luke to use as weapons.

"What about me?" Cleo said.

The vampire pulled an old-fashioned mahogany hat stand from his cloak and handed it over.

"Great!" scoffed the mummy. But there was no time to argue as the mother yeti clambered up off the narrow ledge with ease, her baby clinging

tightly to her thick, matted fur. She threw her head back and shrieked with rage.

GRRRRAAAAWWWLLL!

Resus cricked his neck from side to side. "Bring it on, furball!"

The baby yeti dropped to the ground and scurried toward the children, its mother stomping close behind. The trio tightened their grips on their respective weapons. Then another growl rang out, a new sound from the opposite direction.

GROOWL!

Luke spun around. A second adult yeti—this one shorter and draped in strips of ragged material—was approaching. They were trapped! The two adult yetis glared at each other across the stone circle, ignoring the children between them.

The second yeti darted forward, screaming at the top of its voice.

RAAAAGGGGHHHH!

The baby yeti yelped, and incredibly the mother also appeared to be frightened by the cry. Suddenly she scooped her baby up into her arms and leaped off the edge of the cliff, back down onto the ledge below.

Cleo turned to stare at the victorious newcomer. "What happened there?"

"No idea . . ." breathed Resus. "I thought they were going to eat us!"

"This one still might," Luke pointed out. "From the way it scared off the competition, I'd say it must be the dominant male."

Then, to everyone's amazement, the yeti spoke. "Nah," it said. "I just happen to speak the bingo."

"Bingo?" questioned Resus. "Do you mean *lingo*?"

 16

"Oh, yeah—lingo!" The figure reached up and pulled off a yeti mask to reveal a familiar—if rotting— face underneath. It was a zombie.

"Twonk!" cried Cleo, dashing over and hugging their rescuer. "What are *you* doing here?"

The zombie grinned. "I'm with Vein," he explained, removing a pair of hairy gloves. "I guess you could say that I'm his personal persistent."

"I think you mean personal *assistant*," Luke corrected. He couldn't help but smile. Twonk had been the drummer in Vein's band, and it was reassuring to see such a friendly face in this desolate part of the world.

"Vein's just the person we're looking for," said Resus. "I'm guessing his cave isn't far from here, then?"

"Just on the other side of that ridge," replied Twonk, pointing up to the peak above them. "I heard screaming and came down to see what was happening."

"In full yeti gear," Cleo added with a laugh. "It was incredible the way you frightened those monsters away!"

The zombie's green cheeks blushed purple. "Oh, it was nothing." He smiled. "I just told them you were here to kill them for their fur."

"What?" Cleo gasped.

Resus rolled his eyes. "It was just a trick to get rid of them, softy," he cried. "Or maybe you'd like Twonk to call them back so we can explain that we aren't really after their fur, and we could actually be quite nutritious. . . ."

"Ha, ha," retorted Cleo. "Although I don't know why they wanted to attack us in the first place."

"It could be because you've invaded their territory," Twonk suggested. "You're standing in their nest."

Luke looked around him. "Their nest?"

Twonk nodded, beginning to lead the way up the path. "Circle of stones; dead leaves to keep off the cold. A classic yeti nest."

"How do you know all this stuff?" Cleo asked as the trio followed the zombie.

"I'm supposed to control the crowds of people here to ask Vein for advice," Twonk replied. "But there haven't been any. In fact, there's been no one, really. Just the yetis. So I started to sturdy them—"

"Do you mean *study* them?" Luke interjected.

"Oh, yeah," the zombie said with a chuckle. "Study them! Before long, I was able to copy their sounds—and I made this disguise out of bits of leftover fur so I could get up close to watch them. They're amazing!"

"They're ugly," Resus countered.

"Not at all," said Twonk with a frown. "I find the mother yetis in particular very elegant and graceful."

Soon the group arrived at a flat expanse of rock and found themselves facing the entrance to a small cave. "Here we are," announced Twonk, coming to a stop. "Vein's new residue!"

"Come on, then," said Cleo, heading for the cave. "What are we waiting for?"

Twonk quickly stepped in front of her. "I, uh . . . can't let you in like this."

Luke frowned. "What do you mean?"

"Vein told me to tell anyone who comes to visit that, um . . ." He pulled a crumpled piece of paper from his pocket and began to read.

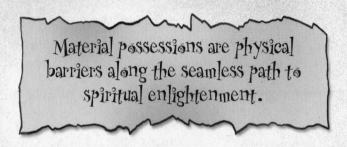

Material possessions are physical barriers along the seamless path to spiritual enlightenment.

"Are those lyrics from one of his flesh-metal songs?" asked Resus, nonplussed.

"It means he wants us to leave all our stuff outside," Luke translated.

"Sorry," said Twonk. "Vein won't allow you to take anything into the cave."

"Anything?" asked Cleo. "What about our jackets and stuff?"

Twonk shook his head. "Indoor clothes only, I'm afraid—and that's an improvement. It took me ages to talk him out of nudie Tuesdays."

"Just what we need," Resus remarked as Cleo and Luke bent to untie their hiking boots. "A weird zombie guru with a dress code!"

Cleo pulled her sweater over her head. "OK, then," she said. "Let's go."

"We can't yet," said Luke, looking pointedly at Resus's cape.

"What?" demanded the vampire. "I'm cold!"

"But there's a mountain of 'material possessions' inside your cape," Luke reminded him.

Resus unclipped his cloak with a scowl and dropped it onto the pile of jackets and sweaters. "If that goes missing, I won't be happy," he grumbled. Shivering, he led the way into the dark interior of the cave.

Meanwhile, behind him, the baby yeti darted out from a nearby boulder. Spying the pile of clothes, it moved closer to the cave. Then, with a bound, it leaped onto the pile and burrowed deep into Resus's cape.

Chapter Three
The Cave

The mouth of the cave gave way to a tunnel that twisted and turned before opening up into a large chamber. Coarse straw mats covered the stone floor, and the room was lit by dozens of misshapen yellow and brown candles. Their flickering flames cast eerie shadows on the rough stone walls.

Cleo pulled her bandages up to cover her nose. "*Eurgh,* what's that smell?"

"I think it's the candles," said Resus, leaning in to sniff. "It's either loganberry or sycamore. . . ."

"It's neither," Twonk informed him. "It's earwax."

Resus quickly pulled away. *"What?"*

"Vein makes the candles himself," Twonk explained. "Each one takes a week or so of digging around inside his ears—although sometimes he needs my wax, too. He says it's nature's way of providing him with light."

"Nature's way of making me vomit, more like," groaned Resus. "Why's he making candles out of earwax?"

"I did try to buy him some nicer-smelling ones from the village," said Twonk. "But he started on about material possessions again."

"Where is Vein, anyway?" asked Luke. "We need to give something back to—"

His words were interrupted by a light jangling sound. A tall figure appeared in the shadows at the back of the cavern and began to dance toward them. He was dressed in ragged white robes and shaking a homemade tambourine.

Twonk dropped to his knees and bowed his head toward his master. "Please welcome the all-knowing zombie emu."

"I think you mean zombie *guru*. . . ."

"Oh, yeah." Twonk grinned. "Guru!"

The figure stopped a short distance away and continued to dance awkwardly on the spot.

"He won't come any closer unless you kneel down and bow," Twonk hissed.

Resus snorted. "If he thinks I'm going to—" Luke elbowed him in the ribs, and reluctantly the vampire sank to his knees beside his friends. The figure danced closer.

"Vein will now shower you with his wisdom," Twonk announced.

Resus glanced up at the nearest candle. "When it comes to being showered, it's not his wisdom I'm worried about. . . ."

Vein shook his tambourine over each of the children in turn. It appeared to be made from a piece of human skin stretched over a jawbone. Finger joints and knuckles were tied around the edge, and they clattered together musically.

Finally, Vein sat down cross-legged on one of the reed mats and gestured for his visitors to do

the same. His green skin glowed eerily in the flickering candlelight, and his jet-black eyes reflected the yellow flames. Cleo shuddered as she remembered that Vein injected ink into his decomposing eyeballs to give the impression of always wearing sunglasses.

Luke cleared his throat. "Vein, we have traveled—"

But the zombie lifted a rotting hand to stop him. Then he smiled, revealing his three or four remaining teeth, and began to grunt, "Oo ah um a onn ay . . ."

"'You have come a long way . . .'" translated Twonk.

"We have," agreed Cleo.

"Or ur-ee a een i-i-ul . . ."

"'Your journey has been difficult,'" said Twonk.

Luke pictured the moment the mother yeti had clambered onto the narrow mountain ledge. "You could say that."

Vein's eyes twinkled in the light of the flames. "U oo a eh-al ee-on or u-in oo ee ee oo-ay, a-eh oo?"

Twonk looked blank.

"U oo a eh-al ee-on?" repeated Vein.

"Um, I don't know exactly," Twonk admitted with a shrug. "I think it's about half past two . . ."

Resus sighed. "As much fun as it is playing Guess What the Loony's Saying, don't you think it would be easier for us to just give Vein back his tongue?"

Luke pulled the matchbox out of his pocket and

slid it open to reveal a lump of diseased flesh. "We are very grateful for your gift," he said, addressing the zombie guru, "but we now have to return all the founding fathers' relics. You see, there's a doorway leading out of Scream Street that—"

Vein pointed excitedly at the matchbox. "A-eria oh-eh-on! A-eria oh-eh-on!"

"'Material possession! Material possession!'" said Twonk, decoding the grunts.

"It's *not* a material possession," said Luke. "It's your tongue!" He pulled a mini sewing kit from the other pocket of his jeans. "Now, who wants to do the honors?"

"Where's Cleo?" asked Resus, emerging from the cave and collecting his cape from the pile of coats and sweaters.

"Washing her hands in a little stream over there," said Luke, pointing. "She said that sewing Vein's tongue back in was the most disgusting thing she's ever done."

"And that's from someone who takes her internal organs out of the fridge once a week to clean them," said Resus. He clipped his cape back around his neck and pulled it across his shoulders.

Shrugging uncomfortably, he re-adjusted it with a frown.

"What's the matter?" asked Luke.

"Dunno," replied Resus. "It just doesn't *feel* right. . . . Heavier, somehow."

"That will be the weight of your material possessions," announced a voice from the entrance to the cave. The boys turned to see Vein striding toward them. "You should cast them aside, and then you may float upon the clouds."

"His tongue seems to be working," muttered Resus.

"Indeed it is!" exclaimed Vein. "And now that I have it back, I can foretell your future."

"No, you can't," said Resus. "That's impossible."

"Don't let Cleo hear you say that," Luke remarked.

"I don't care who hears me," Resus continued firmly. "Fortune-telling is a sham."

Vein's eyes widened. "Then how can I see there is a long journey ahead?"

Resus shrugged. "Probably because you know we have to climb all the way back down this mountain to get to the Hex Hatch."

The zombie scowled. "I predict you will be confronted by danger—"

"Not if we can avoid the yetis," said Resus. "Come on, admit it: there's nothing you can 'predict' that you couldn't easily have guessed . . ."

"Oh, really?" Vein said with a smirk.

"Yes, really!" Resus retorted.

"You shall cross to another place," said Vein, striding closer.

"Yep," agreed Resus, taking a step forward himself. "Through the Hex Hatch and back onto Scream Street."

Now the two of them stood face-to-face.

"You will meet an old acquaintance in a new guise—"

"Zeal Chillchase is a shapeshifter—he could look like *anything* by the time we get home."

"Many strangers will surround you."

"Scream Street's full of normals!"

"Another wishes you harm."

"Sir Otto will do anything to stop us from closing the doorway, as you well know!"

Vein paused for a moment before producing his trump card. "You're wearing underpants with kittens on them!"

There was a moment's silence, broken by Cleo, who had just at that moment reappeared. "Are you?" she asked.

"It doesn't matter!" cried Resus, pulling his cape tighter around his shoulders. "Anyone can stand around dressed in a sheet and guess things—but it doesn't mean they can predict the future!" With a final glare at the zombie soothsayer, he turned and stomped off down the mountain path.

"I appear to have upset your friend," said Vein as Luke zipped up his coat.

"He's just the skeptical type," Luke replied. "He probably wouldn't believe in vampires if he didn't have to brush his fangs in the mirror each morning."

Vein's brow furrowed. "I thought vampires didn't have reflections."

"It's a long story . . ." Cleo said with a smile.

"We'd better catch up with him," said Luke. "Thanks for taking back your tongue."

"My pleasure," the zombie assured them. "I'm glad to have been some use to you. But, please—heed the warnings I imparted to your vampire friend. You shall cross to another world and face great danger."

"We'll bear it in mind," said Luke. "Thanks again for—"

"That's not all," Vein interrupted. "Someone will be seriously injured, and it will affect them for the rest of their life."

"Injured?" Cleo gasped. "Who?"

"That I cannot see," Vein admitted. "All I can tell you is that the solution to your problems will be a knockout."

"Sounds exciting," lied Luke, eager to get away. "And we promise to be careful." Then with a final wave to Twonk, he and Cleo turned to follow Resus down the mountain. Once they were out of earshot, Luke said softly, "I'm worried . . ."

"What about?" asked the mummy. "That Vein's right? That one of us is going to get injured?"

"Partly," Luke replied. "But more that Resus didn't deny he was wearing kitten underpants."

Chapter Four
The Visitor

When Luke, Resus, and Cleo stepped
through the Hex Hatch and back onto Scream
Street, they found Zeal Chillchase standing there
disguised as a stone gargoyle.

"There you go," proclaimed Resus. "My fortune-telling abilities are every bit as good as Vein's! 'You will meet an old acquaintance in a new guise,' my fangs!"

There was a sound like milk being poured into a glass as Chillchase changed back to his usual shape. A pigeon that had been perched on top of the statue's head flapped away in surprise. "The deception was necessary to avoid the prying eyes of the normals," explained the Tracker.

Cleo peered over the hedge. Zeal had opened the Hex Hatch in a secluded yard, but there was always the possibility a nosy tourist would spot the shimmering window in the air. "You stood guard all this time? We've been gone for almost a whole day!"

"I couldn't risk the Hex Hatch being dis-covered," the Tracker replied. "Several normals came this way, but they turned back when they found an oversize garden ornament blocking their path."

"You can close it now," said Luke. "Vein took his tongue back with no trouble."

"No trouble?" said Resus scornfully. "You

mean apart from the freezing cold, vicious yetis, and a seriously deluded zombie?" He pulled at his cape. "And I don't know why this thing's so uncomfortable all of a sudden!"

"Maybe so you'll still have something to moan about?" suggested Cleo. "You've had a face like a goblin licking bile off a thistle ever since we left the cave!"

"I just don't see why Vein has to live at the top of a mountain," grumbled Resus. "Could he have made it any harder for us to give him back his tongue?"

"It wasn't easy," Luke agreed, "but the point is that we *did* give back the tongue." He turned to Zeal Chillchase. "Four relics down, two to go."

"I know," said the Tracker. "Sir Otto flew into a rage when the purple arch over the doorway exploded and the entrance to Scream Street shrank even more. He's been searching for the three of you ever since."

"And now he's found you," snarled a voice. The landlord was storming across the lawn toward them, chewing on a thick cigar. "You're not the only shapeshifter around these parts, Chillchase!" The startled pigeon landed back in

the yard beside the group and suddenly began
to grow, its wings stretching into gangly arms
and its gray feathers melting away to reveal lank
red hair.

"Dixon!"
exclaimed Resus.

"Hi, guys!" cried Sir Otto's nephew when
he had returned to his own form. "How was
your trip?"

Sir Otto rounded on his nephew. "WHAT ARE YOU DOING?" he shouted, blowing clouds of stinking cigar smoke into his face.

Dixon shrugged. "I just wanted to know if they'd had a good time," he said. "It doesn't cost anything to be polite."

"No," bellowed Sneer, "but these three are costing me thousands by returning those blasted relics! People are already having to stoop as they enter Scream Street. At this rate, all the visitors will end up with bad backs. Then they'll never come back!"

"Maybe you should just give up and admit that we've won," suggested Luke.

"Never!" Sir Otto snarled. "I'll milk this odd-ball community for every penny I can get! It's about time you freaks started paying your way."

Zeal Chillchase stepped in front of Luke. "This is *not* the kind of behavior G.H.O.U.L. expects from its landlords," he growled.

"And what are you going to do about it?" Sneer responded. "You can't tell G.H.O.U.L. what I'm up to, or they'll find out that you've been helping the same children who opened the doorway out of Scream Street in the first place!"

A scream rang out from the direction of the central square.

Zeal Chillchase steadied the half-closed Hex Hatch, then strode up to the landlord. "You're going too far, Sneer," he spat. "Those normals are innocent."

Sir Otto pulled a large handkerchief from his pocket and used it to cover the ragged remains of his throat. "Those normals are paying customers," he rumbled as more screams filled the air. "And I think I'm about to raise the price of admission!" With a final smirk, he turned and marched out of the yard, Dixon at his heels.

"What do we do now?" asked Cleo.

Chillchase turned back to the sliver of light in the air behind him—all that remained of the Hex Hatch—and began to expand it with his fingers. "I'll have to keep this open until you can find a way to bring the yeti back here."

"Any idea how we can do that?" asked Resus.

"Judging by the way she wolfed down Sir Otto's scarf and that gnome, I'd say she was pretty

The Tracker glared at Sir Otto for a moment, then without another word he turned away and readied himself to close the Hex Hatch.

"You see?" spat the landlord. "There's absolutely nothing you can do."

"We'll stop you," said Cleo, sticking out her tongue. "Scream Street will be peaceful again before long."

GRRRRAAAAWWWLLL!

Just as Cleo finished speaking, a vicious growl sounded and the mother yeti burst through the closing Hex Hatch. Before Chillchase could respond, the creature picked him up off the ground and threw him across the yard.

GRRRRAAAAWWWLLL!

The yeti sniffed at the air and caught the stench of Sir Otto's pungent cigar. With a disgusted howl, it lashed out at the landlord with a huge paw, sending him crashing back into the hedge. The white silk scarf he always wore around his neck was torn away, revealing strips of damaged flesh—all that was left of Sir Otto's throat as the result of a boyhood injury.

The yeti loomed over the landlord, glaring down at him and chewing on the stolen scarf.

GRRRRAAAAWWWLLL!

"Ge-ge-ge-get away from my uncle," stammered Dixon, and the yeti spun around and began to advance on him instead. The landlord's nephew backed away, trembling. Then he tripped over a garden gnome and crashed to the ground. The yeti pounced.

Dixon screwed up his eyes, waiting for the impact, but the creature ignored him and scooped up the gnome instead. She paused briefly to peer at the figure's painted features, then stuffed it between her jaws and began to crunch loudly.

"And I thought my dad was a noisy eater," whispered Resus.

The yeti roared again—*GRRRAAAWWLL!*—then leaped over Sir Otto and chewed an exit through the hedge before disappearing off down the street.

Silence descended on the yard.

"What *was* that?" squeaked Dixon, finally opening his eyes.

Sir Otto climbed to his feet. He was smiling. "That, Dixon," he said, "was money!"

His nephew looked confused. "Are you sure?" he asked. "I've never seen my pocket change act like that. . . ."

"Think about it," said the landlord. "These little freaks won't close the doorway while there's a yeti loose in Scream Street—there's no way the normals could escape its clutches."

hungry," replied Luke. "Maybe we can find some food and lure her back this way?"

"It's got to be worth a try," said Cleo. "She must be looking for something to—"

She stopped as another furry creature jumped through the half-closed Hex Hatch and into the yard. Dull eyes peered anxiously through a mask of thick gray hair.

"This one's going nowhere!" growled Chillchase, grabbing a lawn chair and raising it above his head.

"STOP!" yelled Luke.

"That's not a real yeti," added Cleo. "It's Twonk!"

The zombie pulled off his yeti mask and stared up at the furious Tracker. "Phew! Thanks, guys!" He grinned. "I thought I was going to get cobblered there!"

"Cobblered?" said Zeal Chillchase, cautiously lowering the chair.

"Don't ask," said Resus.

"What are you doing here?" Luke asked the zombie.

"I saw the mother yeti follow you down the

41

mountain," Twonk replied. "I wanted to try to stop her before she caught up with you, but I was too late."

"The mother followed us?" said Cleo. "Why would she do that?"

Twonk looked sternly at the trio. "Because one of you has kidnapped her baby!"

"Are you out of your tiny zombie mind?" cried Resus. "You think one of *us* has kidnapped the baby yeti?"

"It's the only reason why a mother would travel so far from her nest," Twonk insisted. He leaned in to Resus and sniffed. "Besides, you *smell* like a yeti."

"And *you* smell like rotting flesh and earwax," retorted Resus, "but I'm not accusing you of having shoplifted Vein!"

"Calm down," said Luke. "I'm sure we can get to the bottom of this." He turned to the concerned zombie. "The baby's not here—just the mother." As he finished speaking, a terrified scream could be heard in the distance. "And we'd better get her back as quickly as possible," he added.

"Right," said Cleo. "You're the expert, Twonk. How do we lure an adult yeti back to the Hex Hatch?"

Twonk scratched his head, accidentally pulling out a large clump of hair as he did so. "The cries of her baby should bring her running."

"We've already told you," said Resus. "We don't *have* her baby!"

"In that case, I could try to *sound* like her baby," Twonk suggested. "Perhaps that will trick her." He screwed up his face and let out a series of high-pitched growls.

Grrll! Grrll!

"That sounds just like the little yeti!" exclaimed Cleo.

"Thanks," said Twonk, blushing. "I've been working on that for a while."

"But I'm guessing you'd have to be close to the mother for it to work," said Luke.

Twonk nodded. "She mustn't see me, though. Yetis aren't stupid—if she realizes she's being tricked, it will only make her angrier."

"This could take some time." Resus sighed.

"Time we don't have," Zeal Chillchase stated, having finally stabilized the window to Tibet. "This Hex Hatch has already been open for twenty-three hours—another hour and its energy signature will automatically register itself at G.H.O.U.L. headquarters."

"Why would it do that?" asked Cleo.

"To prevent Trackers from forgetting to close Hex Hatches they've opened," replied Chillchase. "And also to stop rogue Trackers from acting without G.H.O.U.L.'s permission."

"Like you're doing for us," Luke put in.

Chillchase nodded. "If G.H.O.U.L. were to discover what we're doing, they'd take a dim view of my actions."

"But surely all you have to do is close this Hex Hatch and open another one," said Resus.

"That'll start the twenty-four-hour countdown all over again, and we'll be in the clear."

"Unfortunately, that's not possible," replied Zeal. "Holding this Hex Hatch open for so long has seriously sapped my powers. I can keep this one active for another hour, but it will be days before I have the strength to open a new one."

"OK," said Resus. "Then we've got an hour in which to find the baby yeti and get him and his mom back through *this* Hex Hatch."

"We'd better get a move on," said Luke, slipping off his thick jacket.

Zeal Chillchase fished a silver pocket watch from his leather coat and handed it to him. "This will tell you how long you have left before the Hex Hatch needs to close," he explained.

Luke took the watch and studied it. "One hour and six minutes to go," he told the others.

"Then there's no point in us hanging around here," announced Cleo, making her way over to the gap in the hedge. "Come on." Luke, Resus, and Twonk followed her out of the yard and into the street.

Scream Street's central square was packed with normals and residents alike. Everyone was

clumped together in groups, talking in hushed whispers. Huge footprints could be seen on the ground, and an old Transylvanian oak tree had a piece of trunk bitten out of it. Saliva still dribbled down the pale bark.

In the middle of the square, Sir Otto was parading up and down beside the doorway to Luke's world, shouting like a circus ringmaster. "Step right up! See the latest atrocious attraction Scream Street has to offer. You *can* believe your eyes — that creature was the real Abominable Snowman! While this dangerous display lasts, the cost of your visit is doubled — tripled if you're lucky enough to be bitten by the yeti!"

"Just when I think he can't get any worse," grunted Cleo. "Surely no one's going to pay extra for the chance to be attacked by a yeti."

"Don't be so sure." Luke sighed as tourists eagerly surrounded the landlord.

"Which way do you think the mother went?" asked Twonk.

"No idea," replied Resus. "But I can see someone who might be able to tell us. . . ." He dodged through the crowds to where he had spotted his parents in deep discussion with Doug,

one of the street's resident zombies. The others trooped along behind him. "What happened here?" he asked.

"It was such a shock," said Bella Negative. "This *thing* just bounded across the square, knocking people over and biting anything it could reach!"

Doug shook his head in disbelief. "That furry dude had a bad case of the munchies, man. What in the world was it?"

"It was a yeti," said Alston. "I haven't seen one of those on Scream Street since—well, since I was first dating Bella."

Resus's mom's cheeks flushed slightly. "That's right." She giggled, fluttering her eyelashes. "You were so brave back then. . . ."

"I'm still brave now," insisted Alston, putting his arm around his wife. "I could save you from that big, bad yeti anytime I wanted!" He planted a kiss on Bella's ruby-red lips.

Doug grinned, revealing a family of wood lice squirming happily around his teeth. "The vampires are getting their love on, dudes."

"Yes," said Resus, "and I'd be grateful if they'd stop before one of us throws up!"

"Did you see which way the yeti went?" Cleo asked Doug.

As if in answer, a loud crash came from the direction of Everwell's Emporium.

"Don't worry." Luke grinned. "I think we've found it!" And he, Resus, Cleo, and Twonk set off at a run toward the general store.

"Be careful!" Alston yelled after them.

The group crashed in through the doors of the emporium and skidded to a halt. The place was trashed. Shelving units had been toppled and ornaments broken. Pictures had been torn down, and the shop counter had had a huge bite taken out of it.

The yeti was nowhere to be seen, and neither was the owner, Eefa Everwell. In fact, the only person in the shop was an elderly banshee clutching a plastic shopping bag. Cleo hurried over to her.

"Excuse me, please, which way did the yeti go?"

The banshee glared down at her, brow furrowed. "WHAT?"

"Did you see the yeti?" Cleo asked. "Which way did it go?"

"WHAT?"

49

Cleo sighed and raised her voice. "WHERE IS THE YETI?"

"WHAT?"

A younger banshee appeared timidly from underneath the counter, her wild, untamed hair bobbing. "She won't be able to answer you," she said. "My grandma's stone deaf."

"You don't say," muttered Resus.

"I've come to stay with her for a while," continued the banshee. "I'm Favel."

"I would stop to say welcome to Scream Street," said Luke, "but we've got a bit of a problem on our hands."

"I noticed," said Favel. "We only came in to get a sleeping potion for my grandma, then a big, furry monster burst in and started eating everything!"

"Where is it now?" asked Twonk.

"The witch who was serving us chased it out the back way. That thing looked pretty dangerous."

"It is," Luke confirmed. "You should take your grandma home and stay inside until we can get rid of it."

Favel nodded, and taking the elderly banshee by the hand, she led her out of the shop.

GRRRRAAAAWWWLLL!

The sound came from the direction of the storeroom.

"The mother yeti's still back there!" exclaimed Cleo. "And Eefa's alone with her!"

Luke turned to Twonk. "Get behind the counter and start making baby yeti sounds. If we can lure her back into the shop, maybe we can keep her contained and away from the normals while we figure out what to do next."

Luke, Resus, and Cleo ducked behind the counter with Twonk, and the zombie began to growl softly.

Grrll! Grrll! Grrll!

GRRRRAAAAWWWLLL!

The mother yeti's cry was louder this time.

"She's coming!" hissed Resus, pulling the metal poker from his cape. "And I'll be ready for her — *Eurgh!*"

"What's the matter?" asked Cleo.

"The poker's covered in some sort of sticky goo," groaned Resus, wiping his hands on his pants. "And it's got teeth marks in it!"

Twonk ran his finger through the clear slime running down the poker and sucked it clean. "That's yeti drool."

"Impossible!" cried Resus. "The only way that could be yeti dribble is if there was a yeti actually inside my . . ." His voice faded away, and there was a pause as everyone looked at him, the truth dawning. "I think I might know where the baby yeti has gone," Resus said quietly, swallowing hard.

Then a giant hairy paw appeared and dragged him over the counter.

Chapter Six

The Exit

Luke jumped to his feet. "Resus!" he cried. The mother yeti was clutching the vampire to her chest, sniffing at him furiously.

Eefa Everwell dashed in from the storeroom, a magic wand directed at the yeti's back. "I'm right behind you, Resus!"

"I *said* he smelled like a yeti!" Twonk proclaimed.

"Well, if he didn't before, he will now," said Cleo.

"It doesn't matter what I smell like," croaked Resus from the yeti's fierce grip. "Will one of you do something before fur-face here takes a bite out of me?"

"She won't hurt you," Twonk assured him. "You smell like her baby. If anything, she'll try to mother you."

"Mother me?"

Twonk nodded. "You know . . . groom you, feed you, teach you to do your business outside the nest. . . ."

Luke and Cleo tried to stifle their giggles as the yeti began to stroke Resus's hair. "Get me away from this thing!" he exclaimed.

"We will," Luke said, "but if we don't get her baby back to replace you, she'll go on the rampage again. Eefa, what spell is loaded into that wand?"

The witch glanced at the word scrawled along the handle. "Levitation."

"Oh, terrific," scoffed Resus. "The sharp-clawed yeti's not quite dangerous enough; let's give it the power of flight as well!"

"I just grabbed the first wand at hand," Eefa retorted. "You don't have long to choose when a snarling Bigfoot is on the rampage."

"Actually, levitation could work," said Luke, glancing up at the ceiling. "It might scare the yeti enough to make her drop Resus."

"This just gets better and better!" wailed the vampire.

"We'll catch you," Luke promised. "Now, are you *sure* the baby is inside your cloak?"

Resus reached his hand into his cape and pulled out a rubber duck. That, too, was chewed to pieces and glistening with drool. "Yep," he said. "It's in there."

"Then that's where we have to go," said Luke.

"Inside Resus's cloak?" exclaimed Cleo. "Will we fit?"

"He once pulled an entire marching band's worth of instruments from it," Luke replied. "I figure he could fit all of Scream Street in there if he wanted to."

GRRRRAAAAWWWLLL?

The yeti held Resus at arm's length and studied him.

"She's beginning to realize that Resus doesn't

look like her baby," said Luke. "We have to act now."

Eefa muttered a spell and fired a long purple spark from the end of the wand, straight into the yeti's back. Instantly, the creature began to float off the ground, kicking wildly.

GRRRRAAAAWWWLLL!

As the yeti's head reached the ceiling, Luke, Cleo, and Twonk hurried to stand directly underneath her.

"OK!" yelled Luke. "Try to wriggle free while she's distracted!"

Resus pressed hard against his captor's chest. With a final glare at the squirming vampire, the terrified beast decided he wasn't her child after all and hurled him across the emporium, where he tore through the threads of a giant dream catcher and crashed to the ground in the middle of a display of cuddly unicorns.

"You said you'd catch me," Resus groaned, sitting up.

"We didn't know she was planning to go for the slam-dunk approach," said Luke, hurrying over. "Now, take off your cape."

The vampire unclipped his cloak and laid it on the shop counter.

"We're really going in there?" breathed Cleo.

Luke pulled Zeal Chillchase's watch from his pocket to check the time. "Fifty-three minutes until the Hex Hatch closes—we don't have a choice," he said. "Have you ever done this before?" he asked Resus.

The vampire shook his head. "Never."

"Why not?" asked Cleo.

"For the same reason you don't unravel your

bandages and go bungee jumping with them," he retorted. "You know it could be dangerous—but you don't know exactly *how* dangerous."

GRRRRAAAAWWWLLL!

"Still, I can think of worse things. . . ." he added.

Luke looked up at the mother yeti, now bouncing off the ceiling like an abandoned helium balloon. "How long will the spell last, Eefa?"

"A couple of hours," the witch replied.

"Perfect," said Luke. "But Twonk, you stay here with Eefa in case the spell fails for any reason. You're the only one around here who knows how to deal with yetis."

The zombie saluted, accidentally smacking himself in the forehead. "You can rust me!" he announced. Then he produced his yeti mask and gloves and passed them to Resus. "These might come in handy," he said.

Luke stood as close as possible to Resus and Cleo. "Ready?" he asked. They nodded, and Luke grabbed the cloak and dragged it over their heads.

The cape fluttered to the shop floor as the trio disappeared.

Luke, Resus, and Cleo made their way cautiously along a corridor lined with soft, blue silk. Open doorways on either side led to spacious rooms, piled high with everything from slide whistles to sofas.

"This," said Cleo, "is officially weird!"

"You're telling me," said Resus, peering into a room filled with paint rollers, dishes, and bicycles. "I thought I'd lost half this stuff!"

"I'm amazed you can find *anything* in here," Luke declared. "How do you know which room everything's in?"

"I don't," admitted Resus. "I just sort of think about what I want—and there it is."

They reached a junction at the end of the corridor. Three identical routes disappeared into the distance ahead of them.

"This place is *huge*!" exclaimed Cleo. "It could take us ages to find the yeti."

"The problem is, we don't have ages," said Luke, checking the watch again. "The Hex Hatch will be closed in less than fifty minutes."

"We could split up," suggested Resus. "Three corridors, three of us . . ."

"My instincts tell me we should stick together,"

Luke replied. "I don't like the idea of one of us getting lost and spending the next few months stuck in here."

"It's a shame we left Twonk behind," said Cleo. "He might have been able to smell which way the baby went." Her eyes lit up as something occurred to her. "You could transform your nose and follow the scent—you've done it before!"

"I already thought of that," said Luke. "It might have worked if we hadn't just passed several rooms full of rotting vegetables and body parts."

"It's not my fault," said Resus. "That's all my pet leech will eat!"

"Well, it's likely to turn my nostrils inside out if I try to use my werewolf nose in here," said Luke. "Although I might be able to *hear* which way the yeti went. . . ."

Closing his eyes, Luke concentrated on transforming just one part of his body—a trick he had increasingly been able to master since moving to Scream Street. Cleo and Resus watched as his ears stretched and slid up to sit on the top of his head.

"Brilliant!" exclaimed Resus once the transformation was complete.

Luke clamped his hands over his furry brown werewolf ears. "Not so loud," he hissed. "These things are sensitive."

He gestured for his friends to stay silent, then stepped into each blue silk tunnel in turn, listening hard. "That's where Dave the leech is at the moment," he said, pointing down the left-hand corridor. "I can hear him sucking on something squelchy. . . ."

"You'll hear someone being sick if you don't shut up," groaned Cleo.

"Nothing down the middle one . . ." continued Luke, ignoring her. "There!" he proclaimed, pointing down the right-hand tunnel. "I can hear the baby yeti's growls echoing at the far end."

"Then let's go," said Resus, leading the way. Luke and Cleo followed, and room by room they searched their way along the corridor. Eventually they came to a dead end—a wall of blue material blocking their way.

"Nothing." Luke sighed. "I could have sworn I'd heard the baby down this way."

"It must have gone somewhere," said Cleo.

"What about down there?" suggested Resus, pointing to where a shaft of light escaped under the cloth wall. He lifted the fabric. "Looks like a way out . . ."

"If the yeti's back in Scream Street, that'll make things a lot easier," Luke observed.

The trio dropped to their knees and crawled

through the gap in the material. As they emerged back out of the cape, they found themselves in an unfamiliar bedroom.

Resus studied their surroundings. "Uh . . . where are we?" he asked.

"Certainly not Everwell's Emporium," replied Cleo. "Someone must have moved the cape while we were in there."

Resus peered out of the bedroom window. "I think it's gone further than that," he said. "It doesn't even look like Scream Street outside—there's a load of market stalls, and the sky's pitch-black."

Luke picked up a copy of *The Terror Times* from the bedside table and peered at it. He paled.

"What's wrong?" asked Resus.

"We're still on Scream Street," Luke replied. "Just not *our* Scream Street . . ."

"What are you talking about?" said Cleo.

Luke turned the newspaper around to show them the date at the top. "Somehow, we've ended up in the year nineteen seventy-one!"

Chapter Seven
The Brothers

"Are you trying to tell me we've traveled back in time?" asked Cleo incredulously. She ran her fingers over the polished surface of the bedside table just to make sure it was real. It was.

"I know it sounds impossible," replied Luke, "but that's how it looks."

Cautiously, Resus used his foot to lift up the

edge of the vampire cape, now lying discarded on the floor. "No," he said firmly. "We can't be in nineteen seventy-one. This is just my cape — not a time machine. . . ."

"It *does* contain a lot of weird stuff," Luke reminded him.

"Yes, but a gateway to the past?"

Cleo sat down on the bed, the frame creaking. "Then how do you explain all this?"

"I don't know!" cried Resus, flustered. "Maybe it's a prank?"

"A prank?" said Luke. "You think someone's gone to all this trouble just to play a practical joke?"

Resus shrugged. "It's still a better explanation than traveling fifty years backward through time!"

Cleo suddenly leaped to her feet again. "*Shh!* Someone's coming."

Footsteps could be heard in the hallway outside the room.

"Quick!" hissed Luke. "Under the bed!"

The trio dropped to the floor and slid under the bed just as the door swung open. They watched as two pairs of legs entered the room.

Each wore dark, flared pants and highly polished shoes.

"There's my cloak!" said a man's voice. "I don't know what it's doing on the floor, though." He picked it up and dropped it onto the bed.

"Maybe someone's been in here," suggested a second voice, also a man's. The trio looked at each other in panic, praying that they wouldn't be discovered.

"In my room?" came the first voice. "Who'd want to come up here?"

"Well," teased the other voice, "I have noticed that someone around here has been getting a lot of attention from a certain Miss Nurmi. . . ."

Luke felt Resus flinch at the name. "You've noticed too?" asked the first voice. "Thank Drac for that—I thought I was imagining it!"

"What, the way she's been fluttering those big, brown eyes at you from across the square? It's obvious, little brother."

Quietly, Resus dragged himself forward so that he could peer out from the end of the bed.

"So, what do you think I should do?" asked the owner of the bedroom.

The second figure sat down on the bed. "You

do what any self-respecting vamp would do — ask her out on a date."

"You think she'd say yes?" the first figure asked, turning to face his brother.

Resus clamped his hand over his mouth to stifle a cry of surprise. Luke shuffled forward to see what he was looking at. He found he could just about see the face of the first man. He was young — maybe in his late teens or early twenties — and sported jet-black hair and sharp fangs. Right away Luke knew who he was.

"There's only one way to find out." The man on the bed tossed the cape to his companion and jumped to his feet. He, too, was a vampire, of around the same age, and he wore small, round spectacles.

Grinning, the first vampire clipped Resus's cape around his neck, and the two men left the room, closing the door behind them.

Neither Luke nor Resus said a word as they climbed out from under the bed. As Cleo joined them, she looked from one to the other. Both boys looked as though they'd seen a ghost.

"What is it?" she demanded.

"Didn't you see who that was?"

Cleo shook her head. "I tried to wriggle forward to join you, but my bandages caught on one of the springs when that guy sat on the bed. I couldn't move."

Still the boys said nothing.

"Well?" cried Cleo. "Don't keep me in suspense. Who was it?"

"He was younger than I ever remember him," said Resus quietly, "but that . . . was my dad."

"No way!"

"It's true," said Luke. "It was a much younger version of Alston Negative."

"*What?*" exclaimed Cleo. "But that's . . . It can't have been your . . ." She took a deep breath. "Then who was the other man—the one who pinned me to the floor?"

"My uncle Insole," replied Resus. "Neither of you have met him; he lives in a G.H.O.U.L. community in Switzerland with his family."

"There has to be another explanation," said Cleo. "It must be a trick. . . ."

Resus shook his head. "It *was* my dad," he said firmly. "Somehow—I don't know how—we've gone back in time. The Miss Nurmi they were talking about is my mom before she got married. Nineteen seventy-one is the year they first met."

Cleo opened and closed her mouth a couple of times, struggling to find something to say. "How old is your dad?" she asked finally. "Your dad now, I mean . . . How old was your dad this morning?"

"He's forty."

"There!" she said. "If this is nineteen seventy-one, then he wouldn't even be born yet!"

Luke's expression brightened. "She's right! Maybe this *is* just a bad joke."

"I wish." Resus sighed. "The thing is, vampires age differently from everyone else. . . ."

Cleo frowned. "Like dogs?"

"What?"

"You know," the mummy continued. "One human year is the equivalent of seven dog years. . . ."

"I suppose," said Resus. "Only with vampires,

 69

it's slower. That could make my dad about the right age."

"Hang on," said Luke. "If vampires age more slowly than everyone else . . . that should make you only two or three years old!"

Cleo grinned. "Maybe we should have let the mother yeti potty-train you after all."

"Ha, ha," retorted Resus. "But I'm not a real vampire, am I? I age just like everyone else."

"That's a shame," Cleo said thoughtfully. "I could have made you a diaper from my spare bandages."

Resus took a deep breath. "Can we all please just forget about the age thing and figure out what we're going to do?"

"OK," said Luke. "We've found out that your cape has powers we didn't know it had. But I'm sure all we need to do is go back inside and retrace our steps until we come back out on our own Scream Street again."

"Nice idea," said Cleo. "But there's one small problem. Didn't Resus's dad take the cape with him when he left?" The boys spun around, scanning the room. The cape was nowhere to be seen.

"Why would he do that?" asked Resus. "Why would he take my cape with him?"

Luke thought for a second. "I heard your dad say that it was *his* cape. Did it belong to him before it was yours?"

"Of course!" said Resus. My mom got him a new one for his birthday a couple of years ago, and he passed his old one on to me."

"Then what if . . . what if the cape still belongs to your dad in the nineteen seventies but belongs to you in our time?"

"What?" demanded Cleo. "Are you trying to say that both Resus and his dad are using the same cape — years apart?" Luke speculated.

"It's the only solution I can think of that doesn't make my brain melt," said Luke.

"You should keep it in the fridge, like me," quipped Cleo.

Resus sat down heavily on the bed. "We need to try to get the cape away from my dad so we can get back inside it."

"Without him seeing us," added Luke. "Who knows what would happen if he met his own ten-year-old son decades before he was due to be born?"

 71

"That's not our only problem," said Cleo, peering out the window.

"What?" asked Luke. He and Resus joined her to gaze down at the busy market in the gaslit square below. Wooden tables and barrows with colorful awnings stood in neat rows, and the place was filled with shoppers and stallholders. Among them, causing people to jump as it scurried by, was a small bundle of gray fur.

It was the baby yeti.

Chapter Eight
The Boy

"Come on!" hissed Luke, heading for the bedroom door. Checking that the corridor was clear, the trio crept down the stairs and darted out the front door. Once they were in the square, they could hear the panicked yells of the residents as the yeti raced about, biting lumps out of table legs and any merchandise it could reach.

"I'd forgotten what it was like living in

permanent night," said Resus, peering up at the dark, cloudy sky above. The only light came from portable gas lamps attached to each market stall.

Cleo nodded. "It'll be years before we break the spell and bring daylight back."

Resus and Cleo made to enter the market, but Luke stopped them. "We need to be careful we don't get recognized," he reminded them.

"It's nineteen seventy-one," said Resus. "No one will recognize us here!"

"No," agreed Luke, "but someone could see us now and then recognize us in the future."

"Good point," said Cleo. "So if, say, Dr. Skully is here now, we can't let him see us, or he'll remember us being here when we get back to our own time."

"Exactly!" said Luke. "We'll need to keep a low profile so we don't—"

"Hello!" said a cheery voice.

Luke turned to see a tubby boy, probably a couple of years older than they were, munching his way through a bar of chocolate. "Hi," Luke replied before turning back to Resus and Cleo. "In every time-travel film I've seen, it can be dangerous if—"

"Who are you?"

Luke turned back to the newcomer. "Sorry?"

"I haven't seen you before," continued the boy. "Who are you?"

"We're . . . nobody," said Resus. "Nobody at all. Forget you've even seen us."

The boy finished the chocolate bar and then produced a lollipop. "Will you be my friends?"

"What?" demanded Resus.

"I said, will you be my friends?"

Cleo smiled politely. "Sorry," she said. "We're not here for long."

The boy's face fell. "So you won't be my friends?" he wailed. "That's mean!" He began to sob loudly, and several passersby glanced in their direction.

"Don't cry!" hissed Cleo. "I didn't mean we wouldn't be your friends—it's just that, uh . . . we're only visiting for a while."

The boy blinked, tears still running down

his cheeks and a bubble of snot expanding from his left nostril. "So you *will* be my friends?"

"Yes, all right," promised Luke. "If it keeps you quiet, we'll be your friends. I'm, er . . . Tom. This is Dick," he said, pointing to Resus. "And the mummy is Harriet."

The boy wiped his nose with the back of his hand before offering it to his new friends to shake. "Pleased to meet you," he said. "My name is Otto! Otto Sneer!"

Resus's eyes widened. "*You're* Otto Sneer?"

The boy sucked on his lollipop and nodded.

"This is awesome!" The vampire grinned.

"It's *not* awesome," hissed Luke. "We're supposed to be keeping away from anyone who might recognize us back in our own time."

"But it's Sir Otto!" exclaimed Resus.

The boy frowned. "*Sir* Otto? What are you talking about?"

"Nothing," Luke replied quickly. "Pay no attention to him. He's crazy!"

There came a loud smash from farther along the row of stalls, accompanied by angry shouting.

"I think the baby's on the move again," said Cleo. "How long have we got?"

Luke checked the watch. "Forty-two minutes," he said. "Let's go."

He grabbed Resus by the arm and pulled him away. The vampire's face was a picture of delight. "That was Otto Sneer!"

"And *that's* the baby yeti," hissed Luke, pulling Resus down behind a stall selling rolls of silky fabric. "Now, get your head together, or we'll run out of time!"

Cleo crouched down to join them, and the trio peered around the edge of the stall. The yeti had overturned a tub of fruit and vegetables and now sat among the spoiled produce, stuffing apples and oranges into its mouth.

Whenever one of the market vendors or customers moved toward the creature, it snarled angrily and gnashed its teeth.

"This is our chance," whispered Luke. "We can catch it while it's busy eating."

Glark! The yeti spat out a mouthful of sprouts.

"*Eurgh*, that's disgusting!" said Resus.

"Why is it disgusting?" asked Cleo. "I've seen you do exactly the same thing at my house when you tried my dad's tulip stew."

"Not the yeti," replied Resus, pointing across the square. "That!" On the opposite side, the young Alston Negative was walking with a beautiful female vampire—Bella Nurmi. He had wrapped his cape around her shoulders, pretending to shield her from the cold, and when he thought no one was looking, he snatched a kiss.

"I think I'm gonna be sick," groaned Resus.

"Will you concentrate on the matter at hand?" demanded Luke. "We have to try to catch the yeti!"

"How?" asked Resus. "I don't fancy grabbing him bare-handed: he's nearly bitten that stall-holder's fingers off twice already."

"It's a pity we don't have your cloak," said

Cleo. "We could have thrown it over the yeti to pin it down."

Luke ran his fingers over a length of white satin that dangled over the edge of the stall they were crouching behind. "Maybe we don't need the cape. . . ."

He quickly unrolled a few yards of the fabric while the stallholder was distracted by the ravenous baby yeti. Resus used one of his fake vampire nails to cut through the material, and soon the trio had a large  square of cloth. They gripped the edges tightly.

"We need to surprise it," said Luke, pulling a length of cord from the stall and slinging it over his shoulder. "If we all dive at the same time, we should be able to capture it and tie it up." Resus and Cleo nodded.

"OK," Luke whispered. "On three. One . . . two . . . th—"

"I can help!" cried a voice, and a pudgy hand appeared beside Luke's, trying to grasp the material. As Otto Sneer pushed forward, he knocked the group over, and all four of them crashed to the ground just inches from the startled baby yeti. The creature hissed in Resus's face, then raced away across the market, growling noisily.

"Well," said Cleo, wiping bits of squashed banana from her bandages, "we certainly surprised it."

"But we didn't *catch* it," growled Luke. He sat up among the vegetables and glared at Otto. "What did you do that for?"

"I was helping," he replied. "I wanted to do something nice for my new friends."

"But we didn't need your help," snapped Luke. "You let the yeti get away! We almost had it, and now it's escaped!"

Otto's bottom lip trembled. "I'm s-s-sorry." He sniffed.

Luke climbed to his feet, his eyes frantically scanning the market for any sign of the creature.

"He's not my friend anymore. . . ." Otto wailed.

Cleo put her arm around the large boy's shoulders and tried to comfort him. "He's still your friend," she said kindly.

"Then why did he shout at me?"

"Because we're running out of time!" Luke said impatiently over his shoulder.

"I know how to cheer you up," Resus said, grinning. He grabbed a carrot from the wreckage of the stall and pushed it into the teenager's mouth, then he bundled up the piece of white satin and wrapped it around Otto's neck like a scarf. "There you go." He beamed. "That's more like the Sneer *we* know."

"I don't get it," croaked Otto, rubbing at his eyes.

Cleo snatched the carrot out of Otto's mouth and glared at Resus. "That's cruel!" she cried.

"Why?" asked Resus. "I stopped him from crying, didn't I?"

"There!" exclaimed Luke. "The yeti's just gone into Everwell's Emporium!"

"*Whose* emporium?" asked Otto, struggling to keep up with the conversation.

Luke ignored him. "Thirty-seven minutes left." He raced off in the direction of Scream Street's

shop, Resus at his heels. Cleo offered the red-faced Otto a friendly smile. "We'll see you later," she promised before chasing after her friends.

The bat perched over the door of the shop let out a screech as the trio burst in. "Wow," breathed Resus. "This is different!"

"You can say that again," whispered Luke. This wasn't the tidy, well-ordered store they were used to. Cardboard boxes and bags covered every inch of the floor, stuffed with everything from crystal balls to model dragons. Dusty shelves bulged with piles of spell parchments and tattered old books.

"I guess Eefa hasn't gotten around to organizing things yet," said Cleo.

"I doubt it will be Eefa who runs the place," Resus said. "Even without her enchantment charm, she can't be old enough to have run this place in nineteen seventy-one."

"Then who do you think—"

Grrll! Grrll! Grrll!

"*Shh!*" whispered Luke. "The yeti's still in here somewhere. . . ."

Resus scanned the chaotic mountains of merchandise. "There could be fifteen of them in here," he pointed out. "It doesn't mean we'd ever find any of them."

"I think we should split up this time," Luke said. "Cleo, you search behind the counter. Resus—the shelves near the window. I'll take the storeroom. And be careful. The yeti is scared—who knows how it might react?"

Cleo climbed over a pile of boxes and crept behind the shop counter. Cautiously, she bent down to see what she could find.

Resus grabbed the edge of a rug that lay draped over a mound of overflowing black bags near the window and began to pull it off them.

Luke sidestepped around a table loaded with inkwells and headed for the dim light of the storeroom.

And that's when the shop erupted into a ball of fire.

Chapter Nine
The Wizard

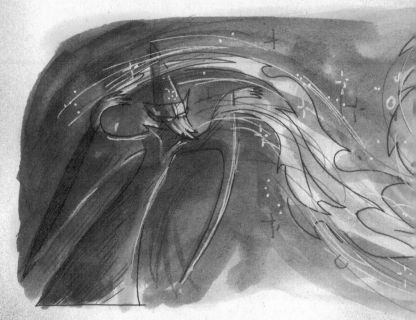

The ball of flame spun around like a fiery tornado, almost reaching the ceiling. The trio pulled back, shielding their faces. Then, as quickly as it had appeared, the fireball died down — leaving an elderly wizard standing in its place. He wore crumpled green robes and a pointed, moth-eaten hat.

"Customers!" he croaked, then immediately launched into a coughing fit. "Sorry about the dramatic entrance there. I was having a bit of a snooze upstairs when I heard the bat. I meant to appear down here in a puff of smoke, but it got a little out of hand. . . ."

Cleo emerged cautiously from behind the counter. "Are you OK?" she asked.

The wizard held up his hand as the last few coughs racked his chest, then turned to smile at her. "Never better, my dear."

"I think you *might* have been better," said Resus. "Your beard's on fire."

The wizard grabbed his beard and peered at the burning hair. Then he snatched a bottle of orange liquid from a nearby shelf and doused the flames with it. He gave a grin as his beard hissed, then he thought to study the label on the bottle and frowned. "Oh, dear," he muttered.

"What's the matter?" asked Cleo.

The wizard gazed at her. "I appear to have coated my beard in jazz juice."

"Jazz juice?"

The wizard nodded. "A concoction—of my own invention—that gives everything it touches the ability to perform free-form jazz. Last week I accidentally washed the dishes with it, and my cutlery kept me awake all night singing the entire back catalog of Courtney Spine. Still, it should be a while before it kicks in. . . ."

Luke decided to step in before the conversation got completely out of hand. "I'm sorry to hear that," he said politely, "but we have a little problem."

"A problem?" repeated the wizard.

"There's a baby yeti loose somewhere in the emporium," Luke explained.

"That's not good," declared the wizard. "We should inform the owner straightaway."

"That's the first sensible thing he's said," Resus muttered under his breath.

"Yes, we must contact the owner without delay. He would want to know that." The wizard

paused, then peered at his reflection in a dusty old mirror. "Wait a minute. . . . *I'm* the owner."

"You are?" said Cleo.

"I think so," replied the strange old man. "Yes, I'm almost certain I am." He held out his hand. "The name's Cuffy." He beamed. "Welcome to Higginbotham's Emporium!"

Cleo took the wizard's hand and shook it. "Thank you. It's very, er . . . nice."

"Is it?" asked Cuffy, gazing around as though seeing the place for the first time. "Yes, yes . . . I suppose it is." He turned to smile at Luke. "Now, you said something about wanting to buy a yeti for your baby. Not a particularly wise choice, if you ask me. They can be quite aggressive creatures — not really suitable as pets. And they eat an awful lot."

"No," said Luke, struggling to contain his irritation. "A baby yeti has escaped, and it's hiding somewhere here in your shop."

"Gosh!" exclaimed Cuffy. "Well, I hope it hasn't come in hoping to pick up some jazz juice — I think I've just thrown the last of it over my beard."

As if on cue, the burnt hair at the end of the wizard's beard began to warble in a tiny voice: *"Skit skat shoo-be-doo!"*

Cuffy jumped, then tucked his beard into the top of his robes to muffle the sound. The bat above the door let out a screech. "Don't you join in," the wizard warned.

Resus shook his head in disbelief. "This can't really be happening. . . ."

"It is," Luke confirmed with a glance at

Chillchase's watch. "And we've only got thirty minutes to go."

Cleo stepped up to the wizard and took his hands in her own. "Cuffy," she said slowly, "we need you to listen to us. . . ."

"Now, listening is something I *can* do!" crowed the wizard. "Along with roller skating—or is it ironing? One of the two."

Cleo continued unperturbed. "We have to find the baby yeti and take it home to its mother."

"Good idea, if you ask me," said Cuffy. "I'd be happy to help—although first I'll need to know who you three are. Can't say I remember seeing you in here before."

"We're, uh . . . visiting our grandma," fibbed Resus, recalling the words of the young banshee earlier that day. "She sent us over to get a sleeping potion for her, and then we noticed the poor baby yeti."

"A sleeping potion, eh?" Cuffy smirked. "Got just the thing right here. . . ." He plucked the now empty jazz-juice bottle from the shelf and peered into it. "Funny, I'm sure this was full a few minutes ago."

"Doo wop de doo!" sang his beard.

Luke sighed and turned to the others. "This is getting us nowhere," he hissed. "Let's just search the shop and see if we can—"

Grrll! Grrll! Grrll!

Cuffy dropped the empty bottle. "What was that?" he demanded. "Something's in here with us!"

"That's what we've been trying to tell you!" cried Luke.

"You have?" said the wizard. "Well, you obviously haven't been trying hard enough. Now, what do you think it might be?"

Luke took a deep breath. "It's a baby yeti," he replied.

"A vicious little gray-haired thing," added Resus. "It's got red eyes, sharp teeth—"

Suddenly, from a nearby pile of boxes, the yeti jumped out and onto Resus's back. "Pretty much like the thing clinging to me right now . . ." The vampire gulped.

The yeti growled angrily in Resus's ear. *Grrll! Grrll! Grrll!*

"Don't move!" hissed Luke.

"Thanks for the tip," grunted Resus, then

he gave a yelp as the yeti dug its claws into his shoulders.

"Does this remind anyone of anything?" asked Cleo.

Cuffy shrugged. "I've been to a few wild parties in my time, but I think I'd remember if we'd ever held a yeti piggyback race—"

"No," said Cleo, "this is exactly like the situation earlier with the mother yeti."

"You're right!" exclaimed Luke. He turned to the wizard. "Cuffy, do you have a levitation spell?"

"I think so," Cuffy replied, and he began to rummage through a shopping bag filled with assorted wands.

"Oh, wonderful." Resus sighed. "I'm about to get slam-dunked again!"

"You might, if anyone could find anything in here," Cleo pointed out.

Cuffy looked up from the bag apologetically. "I'm sorry about the mess," he said. "I don't get many customers now that the market is on three days a week. There's just that nice young man who comes in for his sweets each day. Blotto? Motto?"

"Otto!" corrected Resus. "Now, can you *please* find that levitation spell?"

"Got it!" announced the wizard, pulling a wand from the bag. "Now, what would you like me to use it on?"

"The yeti!" cried Luke. "Make the yeti float up to the ceiling, and maybe it'll drop Resus."

"Good idea," said the wizard.

"Rama-lama-ding-dong!" crooned his beard.

Cuffy pointed the wand at the baby yeti. "OK," he announced. "On three . . . Three!" He activated the spell, and a burst of pink sparks leaped

from the star at the tip of the wand and struck the yeti on its back. Immediately, the creature began to grow, its fangs and claws extending and becoming sharper.

"I thought you said that was a levitation spell!" cried Cleo.

Cuffy squinted at the words inscribed along the handle of the wand. "Nope," he said. "Sorry. This one makes its target double in size. I ordered them so I could try one on a lasagna I'd made. Waste of time, really—I couldn't finish it."

GRRRRAAAAWWWLLL!

With a roar, the enlarged baby yeti finished growing and hurled Resus aside. The vampire crashed into a pile of old copies of *The Terror Times*.

"Ow!" he cried. "That hurt, you overstuffed teddy bear!" As if it could understand the insult, the yeti began to advance on Resus once more.

"Quick!" yelled Cleo. "Someone do something!" Cuffy reached for the bag of wands again, but the mummy grabbed it away. "Maybe we should try a different approach," she said.

Luke spun around, searching for something to distract the yeti long enough to allow Resu

to escape. His eyes fell on a bunch of overripe bananas sitting on the counter. He grabbed one and hurled it at the yeti's feet.

The creature stopped in its tracks and scooped up the banana, stuffing it into its mouth. Then, with a final furious cry—*GRRRRAAAAWWWLLL!*—it smashed through the shopwindow and disappeared out into the square.

Luke and Cleo ran over to where Resus lay. "Are you OK?" asked the mummy.

"I'll be fine once I learn how to bounce," groaned Resus.

"What do we do now?" said Cleo.

"I don't quite believe I'm going to say this," admitted Luke, "but Vein might actually have been right. We're going to have to go for a knockout."

"It's not *exactly* the same," Luke replied. "We didn't have the net last time."

"And the yeti wasn't taller than us last time!"

Luke sighed. "Do you have a better idea?"

Resus shrugged. "Dig a pit and lure the yeti into it?"

"We've only got twenty minutes!" Luke continued laying out the trail of bananas. "No, this is the only way."

"Where are we heading?" asked Cleo.

"How about the front yard of number

Chapter Ten
The Trap

Try as he might, Cuffy just couldn't find the sleeping potion. "It's my own recipe," he said, pulling bottle after bottle from a shelf at the back of the crowded, disorderly store. "Made from an actual dragon's egg."

The trio helped him search. "Are you sure we can't just knock out the yeti with these?" asked Resus, unearthing a pair of boxing gloves.

"Only if you want me to use them on you afterward," warned Cleo. "It's just a baby, remember?"

Resus snorted. "Well, don't ask me to sing it a lullaby!" He found a large net stuffed behind a pile of boxes and pulled it out. "Hey—this could come in handy."

Luke could feel the weight of Zeal Chillchase's watch in his pocket. Time was running out, and Cuffy seemed to be in no hurry at all.

"Anti-bumble liquid . . . Spider's milk . . . Essence of wallpaper . . . Ooh—half a bottle of red wine! I'll keep that for later."

"Are you sure this sleeping potion will work?" asked Resus. "You won't get confused again and hand us something to give the yeti a serrated tongue or the power to shoot lightning bolts out of its eyes?"

Cuffy paused for a second, then hastily pulled a quill and a scrap of paper out of his pocket. "Lightning vision! I like the sound of that one, young man. I bet I could make it by mixing a drop of Lee-Alliston's flouncing gel with half a cup of Drew's combustion powder. The resulting amalgam could then be pushed squarely up the volunteer's—"

"Please!" snapped Luke, pulling out the watch. "We've only got twenty-three minutes

to catch this yeti. Do you actually have any sleeping potion, or not?"

Cuffy put his notes away. "Oh, I've got sleeping potion," he assured Luke. "I inadvertently used it as mouthwash a few weeks ago and spent three days drooling because my tongue had fallen He continued to sift through the assorted and vials. "Now . . . Thinking-aloud cre Concentrated meerkat fluid . . ." He si was certain it was right here, next to the

As the wizard continued to search f Luke grabbed the bunch of bananas counter and whispered to his friends, "Co we're going to have to do this the hard

The market was closing down for t the trio crept among the stalls, leaving bananas behind them. Now that the s lamps had been extinguished, Scream darker than ever.

"Hang on a minute," said Resus af "Let me get this straight. The plan is to what we did before—wait for the and eat something, then jump out at

thirty-one?" suggested Resus, pointing to a house with darkened windows up ahead. "No one will live there until my cousin Kian shows up decades from now."

"And his granddad's still working as the bat above the door in the emporium," Cleo added.

"Perfect," said Luke. "Now, let's just hope the net is strong enough."

"Let's just hope my nerves are strong enough!" quipped Resus.

Cleo opened the gate to 31 Scream Street, and Luke lay more chunks of banana along the path. Then he placed the final piece in the middle of the lawn.

"What now?" asked Resus.

Luke crept into the shadows at the far end of the yard. "We sit here and wait," he replied. "Now that the market's closed, this should be the only food the yeti can smell."

"Let's hope so," said Cleo, checking the watch Luke had given her while he set out the trail. "We've got only seventeen minutes until Zeal Chillchase has to close the Hex Hatch."

Luke sighed. "Talk about a close shave," he breathed. "I never thought we'd—"

"Shh!" said Resus suddenly. "Something's coming. . . ."

The trio strained their ears, and soon they could all hear the shuffling of feet. The steps came in short bursts, punctuated by the sound of satisfied munching.

"It's working," hissed Cleo. "The yeti's following the trail!"

The sounds grew louder and louder as the creature drew nearer, and a few seconds later the gate opened with a soft creak. Silhouetted against the moonlight, the figure padded along the path, stopping every now and again to pick up the pieces of banana and stuff them into its hungry mouth.

Luke tapped Resus on the shoulder. "Get the net ready," he mouthed. The vampire nodded.

Slowly, steadily, they could see the shadow following the line of fruit until it stopped and raised its nose to the air with a sniff. Luke crossed his fingers and hoped that the creature had picked up the scent of the final banana and not that of the three children waiting to pounce.

Resus went to stand up, still clutching the net,

as the figure made its way clumsily across the lawn and peered down at its prize.

Then it spoke.

"Wow, talk about lucky—a whole one!"

The trio looked at one another in alarm. That wasn't the yeti!

Cleo pulled a magic wand from her pocket and prayed that Cuffy had given her one that would cast a beam of light and nothing more. She pointed it at the shadow, and the star at the end began to glow. A moment later, the yard was bathed in golden light and she, Luke, and Resus were able to see who—or what—had been about to devour the bait in their trap.

It was Otto Sneer.

"Hi, guys!" cried the boy, the makeshift white silk scarf still dangling around his neck. "It's me!"

Resus shook his head despairingly. "It's official," he groaned. "Sneer was even more annoying as a kid."

"What are you doing here?" demanded Luke, crossing the lawn toward him.

"I've come to help you catch the yeti," said the boy. "But I didn't realize there'd be something to eat while we worked!" He bent to pick up the last banana.

"They weren't for you," snapped Cleo. "They were supposed to be a trap."

"It's OK." Otto grinned, pulling a large paper bag from his jacket pocket. "I've got loads of candy for that—and these ones are special. They've been soaked in a bottle of sleeping potion that I pinched from the emporium for you."

"So Cuffy *did* have some sleeping potion after all." Resus sighed.

"He's got all sorts of stuff!" Otto smirked. "And because the shop's such a mess, it's really easy to nip in and just take—"

GRRRRAAAAWWWLLL!

The baby yeti—still twice its usual size— suddenly leaped out of a tree above them.

Otto screamed and fell over, candy exploding from his paper bag as the creature landed right on top of him. Luke, Resus, and Cleo could only watch as it began to lash at the terrified boy with its razor-sharp claws.

"Get it off me!" screamed Otto, batting uselessly at the yeti with his fists.

The scent of sugar had driven the oversize

baby into a feeding frenzy, and it snapped its jaws
together again and again, tearing at whatever it
could find.

"We have to do something!" cried Cleo.

Luke snatched the net from Resus and picked
a large rock from the edge of the flower bed.
Wrapping it in the net, he swung it around twice
to gain momentum, then smashed it into the side
of the baby yeti's head.

The creature screeched in anger, and for

a moment Luke thought it was about to turn on him—but instead it leaped off its prey and scurried away, crashing through the gate and disappearing into the night.

Cleo dashed across the lawn and held the wand over the injured boy. The spell was fading fast, but before the light dimmed fully, the trio saw the motionless body of Otto Sneer, blood gushing from the few strips of flesh that were all that remained of his throat.

Chapter Eleven
The Way Home

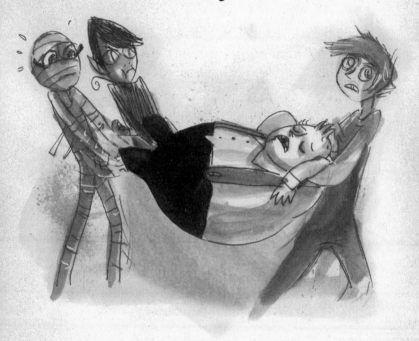

Luke kicked open the doors to the emporium as he, Resus, and Cleo carried the unconscious Otto Sneer inside and laid him on the floor. "We need help!"

Cuffy looked up from his lightning-vision experiment and pulled off his goggles. "I thought you said it was a yeti you were trying to catch. Not my best—well, my only—customer!"

"We almost had the yeti," explained Cleo. "Otto just managed to get in the way somehow."

The wizard knelt beside the injured boy and pulled the stained fabric away from his throat, wincing at what he saw. "He's lost a lot of blood."

"Is there anything you can do?" asked Luke.

"You," instructed Cuffy, turning to Resus. "In the stockroom, third shelf down on the left—you'll find some bottles of blood. Get one." Resus ran to do as he asked.

"Look!" Cleo hissed to Luke. She pointed out of the broken shop window to the deserted square. The yeti, now back to its normal size, staggered around for a moment in the weak moonlight, then slumped to the ground, unconscious. "It looks like you knocked it out after all."

"I didn't hit it that hard," replied Luke. "It must have eaten some of Otto's drugged candy." He pulled the silver watch from his pocket. "Thirteen minutes left," he said. "This is our last chance to take it home."

"You still want to take it back with us?" Cleo asked.

"Yes," said Luke, watching Cuffy as he cleaned blood from the ragged strips of young Otto's throat. "It's too dangerous to leave it here—and we have to save *our* Scream Street from its mother." Cleo nodded, and the pair left the wizard to his work as they raced out into the square.

"I've found the blood!" shouted Resus from the storeroom. "But it's all animal stuff—badger, parrot, rat . . . There's no human!"

"There won't be," Cuffy called back. "I'm getting a blood tap fitted in a few months, but until then, I'm not allowed to keep it."

"Then what do you want me to get?"

"It doesn't matter. I can cast a spell to stop Otto's body from rejecting it."

Resus reappeared with a large flagon of dark red liquid.

"What did you choose?" enquired the wizard.

The vampire peered at the label in the dim light. "Warthog," he replied. "It was the biggest one I could find."

As Cuffy prepared to replace Otto's missing

blood with that from the jar, Luke and Cleo reentered the emporium, carrying the snoring baby yeti between them.

"We finally got him?" said Resus.

"Yep." Luke smiled. "With eleven minutes to spare."

Suddenly, Otto's eyes flickered open and darted around the room. "My friends," he breathed, the air whistling through the flaps of skin at his throat.

"We're here," Cleo reassured him, stepping forward and taking his hand. As she did so, Otto's eyes fell on the yeti, and he began to scream and jerk about in terror.

"Help!" cried Luke, leaning over to try to hold Otto's shoulders down.

Swiftly, Cuffy took a handful of what appeared to be glitter from his pocket and sprinkled it over Otto's face. The injured boy closed his eyes and lay still.

"What did you do?" asked Resus.

"I wiped part of his memory," Cuffy admitted. "The whole past twenty-four hours, if I've got the dose right. He shouldn't remember the yeti—or what it did to him."

"Nothing at all?" asked Cleo.

"Not unless the memory is triggered," replied Cuffy. "Which is highly unlikely; it's a very powerful spell."

Luke looked at Chillchase's watch again. "Nine minutes," he warned.

"We have to go," Resus told Cuffy.

The wizard continued administering the warthog blood to his patient. "I know," he said. "I'll make sure Otto is returned safely to his parents."

"Thank you," Luke said gratefully as Cleo and Resus took the bloodstained piece of cloth and wrapped the snoozing baby yeti in it.

Cuffy looked up at them, his eyes twinkling. "Say hello to the future for me."

Luke gasped. "You know?"

The wizard grinned. "I *always* know."

"Skit skat skiddle-de-doo!" sang his beard.

"Seven minutes," said Luke. He, Resus, and Cleo were crouched behind a low hedge, watching Alston Negative and Bella Nurmi share a tender moment in the moonlight—while sitting on Alston's cloak.

"Do they *ever* stop smooching?" groaned Resus.

"Leave them alone," said Cleo. "It's romantic."

"It's nasty," retorted Resus, plunging his hands into his pants pockets. They alighted upon Twonk's yeti mask and gloves, and Resus broke into a slow grin as an idea occurred to him. "And it could be a little scary, too. . . ."

Alston Negative gave a loud scream as what appeared to be a yeti charged across the lawn toward him and his date. The vampire jumped to his feet and, in his panic, pushed Bella into the creature's path. As he made his escape into the night, Bella gave a squeal and disappeared after him.

Resus pulled off the mask. "I thought my mom said he'd been brave," he scoffed.

Luke laughed as he and Cleo dragged the unconscious baby yeti across the lawn toward the abandoned vampire cloak. "Perhaps running away is considered brave in vampire lore?"

Resus ignored the taunt and stuffed the fake yeti paws back into his pocket. "Still," he said, picking up the vampire cape, "at least they won't be doing any more kissing on *this*!"

"Three minutes!" announced Luke as he, Resus, Cleo, and Twonk left Everwell's Emporium. The sky was still dark, but at least it was *their* dark. They were home.

The journey back through the cape had been uneventful, and the trio had emerged to discover that Twonk had managed to tie a length of rope to the mother yeti's ankle. As the creature was still under the effect of the levitation spell, it looked as though the zombie was sporting a Bigfoot-shaped kite.

GRRRRAAAAWWWLLL! she roared as she bobbed through the air.

"*Shh,*" soothed Cleo. "You'll be home soon."

Bringing up the rear were Resus and Luke, dragging the yeti's baby across the square, still unconscious and wrapped in its cocoon of white fabric. The vampire had clipped his cloak back around his shoulders but was eyeing it nervously as it swished around him.

"I'm not sure I'll ever completely trust this thing again," said Resus.

"It's gotten us out of a lot of awkward situations," Luke reminded him.

"I know," said Resus, "but it's weird to think

that my dad might be wearing it right now in the past!"

"You three really know how to cut it close," declared the Tracker as Cleo swung open the gate to the yard where Zeal Chillchase was waiting.

Luke pulled out the pocket watch for the last time. "Back with both yetis—and ninety seconds to spare," he said beaming.

"What kept you?" asked Chillchase.

"An old friend," answered Cleo as Twonk tugged on the rope and pulled the mother yeti down toward the Hex Hatch. The group could just see the sun beginning to rise over the Tibetan mountainside through the shimmering window.

"We'll be home in time for breakfast," said Twonk.

"I'm afraid not!" announced a voice, and Sir Otto Sneer stepped out of the shadows, Dixon cowering behind him. "That's my main attraction you have there," he snarled, sucking hard on his cigar. "It's going nowhere."

"You made it!" shrieked Cleo with delight, and she flung her arms around the flabbergasted landlord.

"What the blazes?" roared Sneer. "Dixon— get this freak off me!"

The landlord's nephew whispered in Cleo's ear, "I think Sir Uncle Otto wants you to let go of him. . . ."

Cleo released her grip but continued to grin inanely at the bemused Sneer.

Meanwhile, Luke handed the watch back to Zeal Chillchase. Then he turned to Sir Otto. "These yetis are going back to Tibet, where they belong," he insisted.

"Yetis?" demanded Sir Otto. "You mean there's more than one?"

The baby yeti suddenly gave a loud yawn and crawled out groggily from under the piece of white silk.

"Aw, look," smiled Twonk. "It's slippery."

"I think you mean *sleepy*," Resus said with a grin.

"Oh, yeah," said the zombie, blushing. "Sleepy!"

"No—it can't be!"

Everyone turned to see Sir Otto staggering

backward across the lawn, eyes wide as he pointed a shaky finger at the baby yeti. "That's . . . It's not . . ." He gasped, his fingers reaching for the white silk scarf around his throat. Then he turned and ran from the yard, smoke billowing from his cigar.

"Uncle Otto?" Dixon called after him. "Wait for me!"

"I thought Cuffy had wiped his memory," said Resus as the group watched the landlord make his hurried escape.

"Yes, but he did say he might remember if anything was to trigger it," Cleo reminded them. "I guess Little Biter here is just too difficult to forget!"

"Twelve seconds . . ." announced Zeal Chillchase. "Eleven . . . Ten . . ."

Twonk led the mother yeti through the Hex Hatch, and Resus and Luke passed the baby through to him. The zombie turned back and held out a decomposing hand for the trio to shake. "Another adventure with my favorite fiends," he said.

Then the Hex Hatch finally closed, sealing the zombie on the other side of the world with his precious yetis.

Zeal Chillchase slumped to the ground, exhausted, and checked the pocket watch. "Three seconds to spare," he said.

"Sounds like three could be our lucky number," Luke said, smiling.

"Yep," agreed Cleo. "And everything's back exactly where—and when—it should be."

"No, it's not," said Resus, suddenly remembering something. "Twonk forgot his disguise!"

He pulled the yeti mask and gloves from his pants pocket, but as he did so, one of the claws caught in his pants, ripping them and revealing a kitten on the boxer shorts beneath.

Luke and Cleo erupted in laughter as a red-faced Resus struggled to cover them up. Even Zeal Chillchase cracked a sly smile.

Luke put his arm around Resus's shoulders and grinned. "We need to talk. . . ." he said.